For Sarah,
Nick and Helena.
H. P.

★

For Dibbs x
E. S.

First published in the UK in 2021 by Nosy Crow Ltd
The Crow's Nest, 14 Baden Place, Crosby Row
London SE1 1YW

Nosy Crow and associated logos are trademarks and/or registered
trademarks of Nosy Crow Ltd

ISBN: 978 1 78800 977 5

A CIP catalogue record for this book will be available from the British Library.

Printed and bound in Great Britain by Clays Ltd, Elcograf S.p.A.

Papers used by Nosy Crow are made from wood grown in sustainable forests.

MIX
Paper from
responsible sources
FSC® C018072

1 3 5 7 9 10 8 6 4 2
www.nosycrow.com

# A Puppy Called Sparkle

## HELEN PETERS

*illustrated by*
**ELLIE SNOWDON**

nosy
crow

Also by

# HELEN PETERS

**LOOK OUT FOR:**

A Piglet Called Truffle

A Duckling Called Button

A Sheepdog Called Sky

A Kitten Called Holly

A Lamb Called Lucky

A Goat Called Willow

An Otter Called Pebble

An Owl Called Star

A Deer Called Dotty

A Donkey Called Mistletoe

A Foal Called Storm

★

**FOR OLDER READERS:**

The Secret Hen House Theatre

The Farm Beneath the Water

Evie's Ghost

Anna at War

# Chapter One
# I Think There's Something Wrong

Jasmine groaned as her mum turned off the motorway into a service station. It was early evening on the first Saturday of the October half term, and they were returning from visiting Jasmine's sister, Ella, at university.

"Do we have to stop?" Jasmine said. "Can't we just go home?"

"I need to buy a few things for the morning," said Nadia.

"But the animals will be hungry. And they'll be missing me."

Nadia smiled at her as she stopped the car. "Don't worry, they'll be fine. Dad promised to feed them."

Jasmine had a sheepdog, a donkey, a pig, a deer, a sheep and a duck of her own, as well as her two cats. She planned to run a rescue centre when she grew up, and she had already rescued many animals. Luckily, her dad was a farmer and her mum was a vet, and there was plenty of room at Oak Tree Farm.

To Jasmine's relief, it didn't take long to do the shopping. When they got back to the car, she stood leaning against the passenger door while her mum rearranged the boot to make room for the grocery bags. Nadia was a farm vet, so the boot was always full of medicines and equipment.

A few metres away, a woman got out of her car. She was speaking on her phone while scanning the car park as though searching for somebody. She waved at a man a few cars

down and he smiled and walked towards her.

"You must be Diana," he said.

"That's right," said the woman, shaking his hand.

"I'm Chris. Pleased to meet you."

Diana opened the boot of her car and Jasmine glimpsed a dog crate.

"Here she is." She opened the crate and, to Jasmine's delight, took out a tiny, honey-coloured golden retriever puppy.

"Oh!" breathed Jasmine, her face breaking into a smile.

The puppy was gorgeous. She had the sweetest, gentlest face, with dark eyes, floppy ears and big fluffy paws. Jasmine wished she could hold her. She sneaked up closer to get a better look.

Diana handed the puppy to the man. He walked to the front of the car so that he was standing under a lamppost, and looked at the puppy's face. Jasmine frowned. The puppy didn't

look quite well. Her head was tilted to one side at an odd angle and there were strings of white and grey discharge on the surface of her eyes. As Jasmine watched, the puppy shook her head uncomfortably, as though trying to dislodge something.

"What's this gunk in her eyes?" asked Chris. "It doesn't look good."

"Oh, that's nothing to worry about," said the woman. "A lot of puppies have it. She'll grow out of it in a week or two."

The puppy shook her head again. *Something's not right*, thought Jasmine. Mum always said discharge from a puppy's eyes was a serious condition that needed prompt treatment. It wasn't something they would grow out of.

"So I just need the payment and she's yours," said Diana.

The puppy shook her head again. Jasmine wondered if she had an ear infection. She hoped the man would ask about it, but instead he reached into his coat pocket and started to pull out a thick wad of notes. Jasmine stared at the money, amazed. She hadn't realised puppies were so expensive.

He paused with the money halfway out of his pocket.

"You said she's fully vaccinated. You've brought the vaccination certificate?"

"Of course," said Diana.

She took a piece of paper from a folder in the boot and handed it to Chris.

"Jasmine!" called Nadia.

Jasmine walked over to her mum. "Can you come and look at that puppy?" she whispered. "I think there's something wrong, but the lady who's selling her says she's fine."

Nadia glanced at the scene under the lamppost. "She's selling the puppy? Here?"

Jasmine explained what she'd seen and heard. Nadia's face tightened. She strode across to Diana's car. Jasmine followed her.

"Excuse me," Nadia said, smiling at Chris and Diana. "Sorry to interrupt you, but I'm a vet, and I happened to notice that your puppy doesn't look well. I'm sure she's being treated for her eye and ear infections, but I wondered if I could be of any help."

The man looked at her in bewilderment. A flash of fear passed across the woman's face. She put on a smile that was obviously fake.

"I don't think this puppy is any of your business, is it?" she said.

"Is she your puppy?" asked Nadia.

"I'm buying her," said Chris.

"I see," said Nadia. "I assume the mother is here too?"

Chris looked in confusion at Diana.

"The mother is at home with her other puppies," said Diana. "Obviously I couldn't take her away from the rest of the litter."

Nadia turned to Chris. "You know it's illegal to buy a puppy if it's not with its mother?"

He looked startled. "Er…"

"Have you seen this puppy with its mother?"

"Er … Well … no."

"Had you seen the puppy at all before today?"

"Er, no, but—"

"This is ridiculous," said the woman. "You can't just walk up to people in a car park and start interfering in their business. You're clearly mad."

Jasmine had a sudden thought. She crept to the front of the car and stared at the registration number.

Nadia looked at the piece of paper in the man's hand. "That vaccination certificate doesn't look genuine to me," she said. "I think you've been duped into buying a puppy from an illegal puppy farm. This puppy isn't well and I very much doubt whether she's been vaccinated."

"How dare you!" snapped the woman. "You should be locked up, barging in and accusing me like this." She turned and glared at Jasmine. "What are you doing?"

"Nothing," said Jasmine, gazing at Diana with her most innocent expression. She repeated the registration number silently in her head.

"I would strongly advise you," Nadia said to Chris, "not to take the puppy tonight, and at the very least to phone the vet's number on this certificate and check whether it's genuine."

"Will you go away and stop interfering!" spat Diana. "You should be ashamed of yourself, making accusations and causing trouble in a public place."

Nadia didn't move. Jasmine held her breath, her heart beating fast, as the two women stared at each other. The man stood holding the puppy, looking very uncomfortable.

Out of the corner of her eye, Jasmine noticed two police officers, a man and a woman, walking out of the service station. She waved her arms above her head and called, "Excuse me! Hello!"

The police officers looked across. Diana turned and saw them. She froze for a second, and then made a grab for the puppy. The man tightened his hold on her. Nadia stepped between them.

"Come quickly!" Jasmine called to the police. They broke into a run. Diana glanced at them and jumped into her car. She slammed the door,

revved the engine, and with a screech of tyres
reversed out of her parking space and drove
away.

"OY59 7PN," Jasmine said to the
policewoman as she approached. "That's her
registration number."

## Chapter Two
# What Do You Plan To Do?

The police asked Chris lots of questions about Diana and his communications with her. When they turned their attention to Nadia, Jasmine plucked up the courage to ask Chris if she could hold the puppy.

"Sure," he said, barely glancing at her. He seemed stunned by the extraordinary turn of events.

The puppy was warm and soft, and settled quietly in Jasmine's arms. "You're beautiful, aren't you?" murmured Jasmine as she stroked

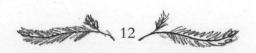

her gently.

The puppy shook her head again. "Poor thing," said Jasmine. "Your ears are hurting, aren't they? Don't worry. Your new owner will take you to the vet tomorrow."

Nadia was giving the police a description of the woman's appearance. "Presumably you can look at the CCTV footage too," she said.

"Unfortunately there aren't any cameras in this car park," said the policewoman. "That's probably why she suggested handing over the puppy here. It's lucky your daughter memorised her registration number."

Nadia smiled proudly at Jasmine. "Well done, Jas. That was excellent thinking."

When the police had taken all the details they needed, they checked with Chris that he was prepared to take responsibility for the puppy, and then they left. Chris turned to Nadia.

"So you think it's got an ear infection as well as dodgy eyes?" he said.

"I can check if you like."

"Will you charge me for it?"

Nadia gave him a scathing look. "Not just to look in her ears, no."

"All right then, if it's not going to take too long. I need to get home."

Nadia fetched her pen torch from the car. Jasmine held the puppy close and stroked her while Nadia shone the torch inside her ear and gently felt around with her fingers. The puppy gave a little yelp and jerked her head away.

"Yes, it's quite red and swollen," said Nadia. "She's definitely got an ear infection. And the head tilt indicates that it might be spreading deeper down, into the middle ear. It will need treating quickly before it gets worse. It must be very painful for her, poor little thing."

"So what's the treatment?" asked Chris.

"I expect the vet will prescribe her some medicated eardrops and an ear cleaning solution," said Nadia.

 14

Chris frowned. "Is that expensive?"

"It can be, I'm afraid. Ear infections can be tricky to manage. Sometimes they need several weeks of treatment. They can be caused by an underlying condition, like  an allergy, so the vet might look into that too."

"That doesn't sound cheap," he said. "And what about her eyes?"

"I can't tell you for certain, but it looks like what we call 'dry eye'. Its official name is KCS – keratoconjunctivitis sicca."

"Is it serious?"

"Well, it's uncomfortable, and if it's not treated promptly it can cause ulcers and other problems."

"Oh, good grief," said Chris. "I don't believe this."

"It might take a few different medications before the vet finds the one that works for her, but I'm sure they'll be able to get her back to full health. In the worst cases, dogs need surgery, but that's only if other medications don't work."

"So it's going to cost a fortune. And then there's the vaccinations. You say you think this is fake?"

He passed the paper to Nadia. She frowned as she scanned the details.

"Yes, this doesn't look like a genuine vaccination record. For a start, it's a photocopy, not an original. The stickers from the vaccine vials should be on the record card, and this just has photocopies of stickers."

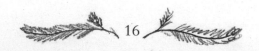

"So Diana lied to me? Does that mean she hasn't been microchipped either? Diana told me she had been."

"I can check now," said Nadia.

She fetched her scanner and ran it over the puppy. There was no sound. She tried again, but the scanner stayed silent. She raised her eyebrows as she looked at Chris.

"So, no microchip?" he said.

"I'm afraid not."

"I don't believe this! That woman sounded so nice on the phone, and now she's landed me with a sick, unvaccinated dog who needs a fortune spent on her."

"Did she ask you to pay a deposit before you saw her?"

"Yes. She said other people were interested, but if I paid a deposit straightaway I could have her."

Nadia sighed. "It looks very much as though she's running a puppy farm."

"A what?"

Jasmine was glad he'd asked because she wanted to know too.

"They're illegal places where puppies are bred in terrible conditions," said Nadia. "Puppy farmers only want to make money, so the mothers are forced to have litter after litter of puppies and the dogs are kept as cheaply as possible. They're often sold with fake vaccination certificates, and the buyers don't find out until it's too late that their puppy has serious health problems."

The man pressed his hand to his forehead. "This is a nightmare. I just wanted a cute puppy for my girlfriend's birthday."

Nadia didn't look impressed. "You should report the seller to the RSPCA, and to their local council. The council will check to see if they're actually licensed to sell puppies, and the RSPCA will inspect them to see how the dogs are being looked after. If it is an illegal puppy

farm, hopefully they'll shut it down and the owners will be prosecuted."

The man held up his hands. "I can't do this. I don't want to be mixed up in anything dodgy. I can't deal with the stress."

"Well, in that case, I'll report them," said Nadia.

"It's not just that. It's the whole thing. I can't deal with a sick, illegal animal."

"So what do you plan to do?"

He looked at the puppy lying in Jasmine's arms. "You're a vet. You take her. Do what you like with her. I don't want any more to do with it."

# Chapter Three
## She's Called Sparkle

Jasmine sat in the car, stroking the tiny puppy on her lap and talking to her softly. Despite her obvious discomfort, the puppy wagged her tail when Jasmine spoke to her.

"I can't believe we went to a service station for bread and milk and came home with a puppy!" she said. "Tom won't believe it."

Tom was Jasmine's best friend, and they had rescued many animals together.

"You know we're not keeping the puppy, don't you?" said Nadia. "I'll ask in the surgery

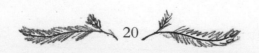

tomorrow; I'm sure one of the other vets or
nurses will take her."

Jasmine hoped they wouldn't, but she kept her
thoughts to herself.

"I need to name her anyway," she said. "Even
if I only have her for a day, I can't just call her
'the puppy'."

"What will you call her?" asked Nadia.

Jasmine studied the puppy's sweet face and
tried out names in her head. They had left
the motorway and were driving along a high
street. Nadia stopped at a red light and Jasmine
looked at a poster in a shop window. "Buy Your
Fireworks Here," it said. There was a picture of
people beside a bonfire, waving sparklers.

"Sparkle!" said Jasmine. "She's called Sparkle."

"Sparkle?" said Nadia. "She looks the
opposite of sparkling to me, poor thing."

"She will be sparkling though. Once you've
treated her and I've cared for her, she'll be the
sparkliest little puppy you've ever seen."

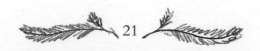

21

Jasmine set her alarm for six o'clock the next morning, but just after half past five she was woken by whining and scrabbling noises. She threw off her covers and knelt down beside Sparkle's crate. The little puppy was jumping up at the bars.

"It's all right, Sparkle, I'm here. Let's go to the garden."

When they had got home the previous evening, Nadia had looked at Sparkle's teeth to find out her age. She estimated that the puppy was between seven and eight weeks old.

"She might go straight to sleep in her crate," she had said, "but if she cries in the night, don't touch her, just talk to her reassuringly and she should soon settle."

They agreed to share the night-time toilet trips, so Jasmine took Sparkle to the garden before she went to bed, and then Nadia took her at midnight and Jasmine at three in the morning.

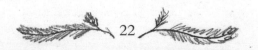

"Come here, Sparkle," said Jasmine now, as she opened the crate door and scooped the warm, soft, wriggly puppy into her arms. She clipped Sparkle's lead on, hurried downstairs and put on her wellies.

She led the puppy to the place at the edge of the garden that she'd chosen as her toilet spot the previous evening. As soon as Sparkle had finished, Jasmine bent down to make a fuss of her.

"Well done, Sparkle! Good girl." She looked closely at the puppy's lovely face.

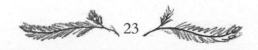

"Your eyes look better today, and I'm sure you're holding your head a bit straighter. The medicines must be working. Let's get your breakfast."

Jasmine fed Sparkle in her crate and then took her out to the garden again. Sparkle was in a playful mood, scampering about and barking for Jasmine's attention, but Jasmine refused to be drawn in. She couldn't wait

to start playing, but she had read all about toilet training a puppy last night, and she was determined to follow the advice.

"We'll play afterwards," she said. "If we start playing now, you'll forget what we're here for, and then you'll have an accident in the house."

When Sparkle had finished, Jasmine praised her lavishly. They went indoors and found Michael, Jasmine's dad, sitting at the kitchen table drinking tea.

"Hello there," he said, smiling at the puppy. "Did she keep you awake all night?"

"No, she was really good. Can you keep an eye on her while I fetch her crate down?"

"With pleasure."

When Jasmine brought the crate into the kitchen, she was thrilled to see Sparkle sitting on Dad's lap. He was stroking her as he drank his tea and read *Farmers Weekly*. If Dad loved Sparkle, that would surely make it easier to persuade him to keep her forever.

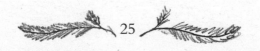

Jasmine set up the crate at the far end of the kitchen, where it would be quieter. Then she picked up the puppy.

"I'm going to see if she can play fetch," she told Dad.

"Well, she's a retriever, so it should come naturally." He took his coat from its peg and went out to the farmyard to start his day's work.

Jasmine knelt on the hall rug and positioned the puppy opposite her. She stroked her head softly.

"This is the ball we're going to use," she said, taking a tennis ball from her pocket. Sparkle

fastened her eyes on it. Jasmine rolled the ball
slowly backwards and forwards on the floor
between her hands. Sparkle's eyes followed it
constantly. After Jasmine had rolled the ball a
few times, Sparkle pounced on it and picked it
up in her mouth.

"Good girl!" said Jasmine, putting her hand
on the ball. Sparkle kept her grip on it, so
Jasmine prised it away from her. Then she rolled
it a little way away. This would teach Sparkle
that even though she had to give up the ball,
she would be allowed to play with it again
straightaway.

Sparkle scampered after the ball. Jasmine had to stop herself from praising her as she went. That might make her come straight back and forget about fetching it.

As soon as Sparkle had the ball in her mouth, Jasmine said, "Good girl!" and Sparkle turned and trotted back to her.

When they had done this a few times, Jasmine started to say, "Fetch!" as she threw the ball. After a while, she noticed her mum standing on the stairs, watching.

"She's doing well," Nadia said.

"She's really clever," said Jasmine. "She learns so fast."

After breakfast, Nadia said she would make her phone calls in the kitchen and keep an eye on Sparkle while Jasmine walked Sky and looked after her other animals. Truffle the pig, Dotty the deer and Mistletoe the donkey all lived together in the big orchard.

"I've got a new friend for you to meet,"

Jasmine told them as she brushed Mistletoe's coat. "She's called Sparkle, and she's so cute and fluffy. I'll bring her out to see you later."

When Jasmine had fed, groomed and mucked out the animals, she went back to see Sparkle. Nadia was on the phone. Jasmine's stomach felt squirmy. Was somebody coming to take Sparkle away already?

The puppy scampered over to Jasmine, wagging her tail. Jasmine scooped her up and took her out to the garden. When they returned, Nadia was finishing a phone call. She gave Jasmine a tired smile.

"You'll be pleased to hear that no one at the surgery can take Sparkle. They've all got homes and gardens full of waifs and strays already, and a puppy's such a lot of work."

Jasmine felt a rush of excitement. "So can we keep her?"

"You know we can't. I'm going to phone the rescue centre."

"No!"

"She'll be very well looked after. They'll treat her infections and they'll find her a good home."

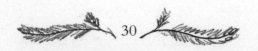

"But she'll be in a cage. She's had a horrible start in life, and the stress of moving into kennels can be really bad for a dog's mental health. I've read about it. And she doesn't need to go to a rescue centre. You can treat her infections here, and then I can look after her."

"Jasmine, you know how much time it takes to look after a puppy. And you're busy enough with your other animals. Plus you're at school for six hours a day. A puppy can't be left for six hours."

"Can't I stay at home? I bet I'd learn a lot more than I do in school."

"You might learn a lot about puppies, but I'm not sure how much else you'd learn."

Jasmine didn't see why she needed to know about anything else, but there was no point saying that to Mum.

"What about a puppy-sitter?" she said. "People have puppy-sitters when they go to work, don't they?"

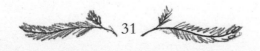

"We can't pay for a puppy-sitter, Jasmine."

"But what if it was someone you didn't have to pay?"

"Like who?"

Jasmine considered all the people she knew, and suddenly the perfect person popped into her head.

"Mrs Thomas!" she said triumphantly.

Mrs Thomas was a friend of theirs. She kept goats, and Jasmine and Tom often visited them after school.

"We can't ask Mrs Thomas to look after a puppy all day," said Nadia. "It wouldn't be fair."

"No, it would be perfect! We were talking about dogs the other day, and she said she loves them but she hasn't got the energy to have one around all the time, and she's too old to get up in the night with a puppy. But this way she'd have a dog to keep her company while I was at school, and I'd have Sparkle the rest of the time."

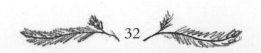

Nadia looked at Jasmine. Then she looked at the puppy. Sparkle gazed back, her head on one side.

"*Please*," said Jasmine. "You know I'd look after her well. I'll learn all about golden retrievers and how to care for them and train them."

Nadia was silent for a minute, gazing at the puppy. Sparkle wagged the tip of her tail.

"Look," said Jasmine. "She's smiling at you."

Nadia turned to her. "I'll phone Mrs Thomas and see what she thinks. If she likes the idea – and only if she does – then maybe we can keep Sparkle for a while."

"Oh, thank you, Mum!"

Nadia left the room to phone Mrs Thomas. Jasmine cuddled Sparkle, her heart beating anxiously.

When Mum came back, she was smiling. "Mrs Thomas said she'd love to be Sparkle's puppy-sitter."

"Oh!" cried Jasmine, hugging the puppy. "Did you hear that, Sparkle? You're going to stay with us!"

"But we're not taking on another dog forever, Jasmine. We're just going to foster her until we find a permanent home. Do you understand?"

"Yes, Mum," said Jasmine. "I understand."

# Chapter Four
# A Full-Time Job

"I think I should introduce Sparkle to Sky now," said Jasmine. "While the house is quiet, before Manu gets back from his sleepover."

"Good idea," said Nadia.

Manu was Jasmine's little brother. When people were being polite about him, they used words like "lively" and "energetic".

"I'll keep Sparkle on her lead," said Nadia, "and you can bring Sky in on his lead."

Sky was resting in his crate in the scullery. He stood up and wagged his tail when Jasmine

came in.

"We're going to meet a new friend," said Jasmine. "You can be like a wise old uncle to her."

The sheepdog was actually quite young, and he had plenty of energy. Jasmine hoped the two dogs would enjoy each other's company. She had put the top she was wearing last night into Sky's crate, so Sky could get used to Sparkle's scent before they met.

She led Sky into the kitchen, where Sparkle was sitting on Mum's lap. Jasmine brought Sky close enough to sniff her, but kept a firm hold on his lead so she could pull him away if necessary.

Sky stretched his head forward to sniff the puppy. Sparkle gazed around as though she wasn't quite sure what she thought of this. Nadia stroked her gently. Jasmine watched both dogs' body language closely for signs of stress. But they were wagging their tails.

"Good boy, Sky," said Jasmine. "Good boy."

They let the dogs get used to each other's presence for a few minutes, and then Nadia lowered Sparkle to the floor, keeping hold of her lead. Sparkle circled Sky, and Sky bent his head to sniff the puppy's tail. She circled Sky a few more times, and then walked towards the collie's face and sniffed his nose.

"Good girl, Sparkle," said Nadia. "That's right, you get to know him."

Sparkle sniffed Sky's underbelly. Jasmine laughed. "You won't find any milk there. Sorry, Sparkle."

The puppy barked excitedly and placed her front legs flat on the floor with her bottom raised and her tail wagging.

"That's a good sign," said Nadia. "She's inviting Sky to play-fight with her."

"They both seem relaxed, don't they?" said Jasmine.

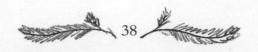

"Yes, I think they'll be fine, but they'll need to be supervised whenever they're together for a while, just to be on the safe side. Always have someone with you, so they can both be on a lead, and make sure they're listening to you even if they're playing together."

A car pulled up in the farmyard. Jasmine glanced out of the window.

"Uh-oh, Manu's back."

"I need to catch Ben's mum before she goes," said Nadia. "Just pop Sky back in the scullery, Jasmine."

Nadia went to the front door and Jasmine opened the scullery door for Sky.

Then she stared in amazement. In the middle of the floor sat a little robin, its feathers all ruffled up. Jasmine glanced at the cats' bed, but luckily it was empty.

"Bed, Sky," said Jasmine, and he walked obediently into his crate. Jasmine shut him in and closed the scullery door. The robin didn't move.

"Poor thing, you must be in shock. Did the cats bring you in? Naughty creatures."

She took a tea towel from the draining board

and lowered it gently over the robin. Then she carefully picked up the tiny bird wrapped in the towel and held it to her chest as she opened the back door. She looked around for a safe place to put the robin out of reach of the cats, until it had recovered enough to fly away.

The big hanging basket on the wall would be perfect. Jasmine set her bundle in the basket, and gently removed the towel. The robin sat motionless.

"You're safe there, little robin. I'll come and check on you in a minute."

As she went back into the scullery, she heard Manu shrieking with laughter. She hurried into the kitchen.

Manu was holding an ice-cream cone, and Sparkle was jumping up at him and licking the ice cream off the cone, her tail wagging madly.

"Leave me some ice cream too!" said Manu. "Here, puppy! Fetch!" He grabbed Sparkle's tennis ball and threw it across the room. It hit

a mug on the dresser. The mug crashed to the
floor and smashed into dozens of pieces. Sparkle
yelped and jumped in fright. A puddle started
forming on the floor beneath her.

"Oh, she's doing a wee!" yelled Manu. "Look,
Jasmine!"

With a murderous look at her brother,
Jasmine scooped up the puppy and hurried to
the garden. Sparkle stopped weeing when she
was picked up, and started again once Jasmine
placed her in her toilet spot.

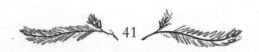

"Good girl, Sparkle," said Jasmine, making a big fuss of her when she finished. She took Sparkle back to the kitchen. Mum opened the door from the scullery at exactly the same time as Jasmine came in from the hall.

"Oh, dear," said Nadia as she saw the puddle. "How did that happen?"

"How do you think? Manu, of course."

"It wasn't my fault!" protested Manu.

"Of course it was your fault. It's always your fault."

"But why weren't you supervising her?" Nadia asked.

"Because of the robin," said Jasmine, and she told Mum what had happened. They went outside and looked in the hanging basket. The robin had gone.

"That's good," said Nadia. "It must have flown away."

"There it is!" said Jasmine. And, sure enough, a little fluffed-up robin was perched on a shrub

across the path.

"Lovely," said Nadia.
"Well done, Jasmine. Now, you'd
better clear up that puddle."

"I can't believe Manu. I've been so careful,
taking her out each hour so she doesn't go in
the house. That article said every accident sets
them back."

"Don't worry. All puppies have accidents once
in a while. Just clean it very thoroughly with the
special cleaner, to get rid of the smell, otherwise
she might go in the same place again."

"And tell Manu he's not allowed to go near
her," said Jasmine. "He's not fit to look after a
puppy."

"It's a good lesson to learn," said Nadia. "You
really can't take your eyes off her for a second.
A puppy is a full-time job."

# Chapter Five
# The Best-Trained Puppy Ever

Jasmine's best friend, Tom, was away for the first week of half term, visiting relatives. So it wasn't until the following Sunday that Jasmine finally got to take Sparkle to meet him.

Tom's cottage bordered Oak Tree Farm, so Jasmine could walk there across the fields. Today, though, Nadia took her in the car.

"I'll be passing Tom's house anyway," she said, "and I'd like to say hello to his mum. I haven't seen her for ages."

Tom's mum, Mel, answered the door.

"What a gorgeous little puppy!" she said. "Tom's told me all about her. I'm sure you won't have any trouble rehoming her, especially with Christmas coming up."

"We're not rehoming her before Christmas," said Nadia. "I'm not going to let her become one of those poor little puppies that get given as Christmas presents and then abandoned because the idiots who buy them have no idea how much work it is to look after a dog."

Mel stared at her, eyes wide. Then she smiled. "I always wondered where Jasmine got her fierceness from. And now I know."

Nadia laughed. "As soon as Christmas is over, though, we're finding a proper home for Sparkle. And that's where I differ from my daughter. If it were up to Jasmine, we'd keep every single animal I treated."

"Have you got time for a coffee?" asked Mel. "Tom's in the garden, Jasmine."

Tom was sitting on the grass, feeding carrot

sticks to his guinea pigs, Snowy and Twiglet. He looked up as Jasmine approached.

"Oh, she's so cute! Hang on, I'll put the guineas back. Come on, boys, into your hutch."

Once the guinea pigs were safely in, Jasmine carried Sparkle over to meet Tom.

"She's the cutest puppy ever!" said Tom, stroking her floppy ears and big soft paws. "She's got such a lovely face."

Jasmine gazed lovingly into Sparkle's dark eyes. "I know. She's the sweetest puppy in the world."

"Can I hold her?"

"Sure." Jasmine handed the warm little bundle to her friend.

"She's beautiful," said Tom. "Do you think your parents might change their minds about keeping her?"

Jasmine sighed as she settled herself cross-legged on the grass. "I don't think so. And I don't think it would be right, really. Sky's fine

because he's a sheepdog, so he's out on the farm all day with Dad, but Dad couldn't have Sparkle with him as well, so she'd be on her own too much."

"But isn't Mrs Thomas puppy-sitting her?"

"She said she'll do it until the Christmas holidays. So we have to find Sparkle a new home by January. She's going to need an owner who can spend loads of time with her. She's really clever, so she gets bored if she's left alone. I've been training her, and she's so quick to learn."

"Let's do some training now," said Tom.

"That would be great. I need to see if she'll still obey me when there are distractions."

"OK, you try getting her to do things and I'll be distracting."

"As long as there haven't been any other dogs here recently," said Jasmine. "She hasn't had her second vaccinations yet, so she could catch horrible diseases from unvaccinated dogs."

Tom shook his head. "There's never any other dogs here."

Jasmine set the puppy down on the lawn. Sparkle trotted around the garden, sniffing first Tom's shoes and then the ground. She ran to the guinea pigs' run, where Snowy and Twiglet were nibbling grass. Sparkle stared at them through the chicken wire. She gave a little bark and the

guinea pigs froze in fear. Jasmine scooped her up, carried her to the bottom of the garden and took a puppy treat from her pocket.

"She can work without treats at home, but I think she might need them here to keep her focused."

She set Sparkle on the ground. The puppy trotted to the hedge and started sniffing it.

"I bet she can smell rabbits," said Tom.

"There's so many round here."

"I wish I had a dog's sense of smell," said Jasmine. "It must be a whole different world for them, detecting all these things we don't even know are there. No wonder they get distracted. Sparkle!"

As if to prove her point, Sparkle ignored her. She was sniffing around the base of a rose bush, her tail wagging.

"Sparkle!" called Jasmine again, but the puppy still ignored her. Jasmine picked her up and showed her the treat. When Sparkle looked at it, Jasmine set the little dog down in front of her. Sparkle stood with her golden tail wagging and her eyes focused on the treat.

Jasmine held it in front of Sparkle's nose and slowly moved it in an arc over the puppy's head. As Sparkle moved her head upwards to keep her eyes on the treat, her bottom naturally moved downwards, until she was sitting on the ground.

"Good dog!" said Jasmine, ruffling her fur and

giving her the treat. Sparkle wolfed it down.

"Don't you ask her to sit when you do it?" said Tom.

"Not at first. When she can do it well, you gradually stop holding the treat and just let her follow your empty fingers. Then you praise her and give her the treat when she sits. And then you start saying 'Sit' before you give the hand signal. Once she's figured out that the word's important, you can fade out the hand signal."

"Won't she get fat if you keep giving her treats?" said Tom.

"They're healthy treats, and you make it part of her daily food allowance, so it's not extra. And I'll gradually stop them and just reward her with attention."

"Can I have a go?"

"Sure." Jasmine handed him a treat and he showed it to Sparkle. Then he moved it in an arc above her head, and Sparkle sat.

"Good girl!" he said, giving her the treat.

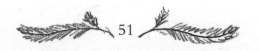

"That's great!" said Jasmine. "She's never sat for anyone except me before. Though Manu's the only one who's tried it, and he's rubbish at dog training. He does it in a different way each time, and he never stops talking, so she gets completely confused about what she's meant to do. Look, I'm teaching her to respond to her name too."

She got Sparkle's attention, showed her a treat and threw it about a metre away. Sparkle ran and crunched it up.

"Sparkle!" called Jasmine, and Sparkle turned and ran back.

"She'll always turn to me when she's finished it, because she wants more," Jasmine said. "So I have to call her just before she turns."

She put a treat on the ground in front of Sparkle. As the puppy ate it, Jasmine called her name and ran a little way away from her. Sparkle finished the treat and ran to her. Jasmine praised her and gave her another one.

"She's quite good at this now, but I need to know she'll come when I call her in a crowded place, or when she's distracted by something."

"I'll kick a ball around," said Tom, "and you call Sparkle."

He kicked a football across the grass. Sparkle raced after it and pounced on it.

"Sparkle!" called Jasmine. But Sparkle was

having far too much fun, patting the ball with her paw and watching, fascinated, as it rolled away. Tom kicked it again and Sparkle ran after it, barking.

"Sparkle!" called Jasmine. The puppy took no notice. She leapt at the moving ball and stopped it with her paws. Jasmine called her again, but Sparkle kept playing with the ball. Tom picked it up and Sparkle rolled over on her back to have her tummy tickled.

Jasmine laughed. "I don't think she's ready yet. I'll take it back a step, then we can practise again with distractions in a day or two."

"Can you come over tomorrow?" asked Tom.

"Sure. I'll bring her every day. It's good for her to meet other people and places. By the end of half term, she'll be the best-trained puppy ever."

# Chapter Six
# How to Spot a Puppy Farm

Jasmine was sad to say goodbye to Sparkle when she and Tom handed her to Mrs Thomas on their first day back at school, but she knew Sparkle would have a lovely time with her new puppy-sitter.

"You're doing your talk this morning, aren't you?" said Tom as they walked up the lane.

Everyone in their class was giving a talk about a topic they had researched over the holiday. Jasmine had volunteered to go first, to get it over with.

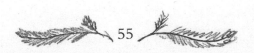

"Yes," she said. "Oh, look, there's Lily and Shadow." She waved at a girl approaching the school from the opposite direction, with a dog on a lead beside her. Lily's mum walked behind them, with Lily's little brother in a pushchair.

Lily had started in Jasmine and Tom's class in September. She loved reading, dance and gymnastics. She had type 1 diabetes, which meant she had to wear a glucose monitor and have regular injections of insulin, but her diabetes didn't stop her from doing anything.

Jasmine had no interest in dance or gymnastics, but she liked Lily, and she especially liked her dog.

"Hi, Shadow," she said, stroking the spaniel's silky ears. "Hi, Lily."

Shadow wore a bright-yellow jacket that said "ASSISTANCE DOG" on one side. On the other side was a circular logo with a drawing of a dog's head and the words: "ALERT DOGS UK".

"Hey, guess what?" said Lily. "Shadow's
coming into school tomorrow!"

"Really?" said Jasmine. "How come?"

"I'm doing my talk on assistance dogs, and
Ms Walker said I could bring him in for it."

"Oh, that will be amazing. I wanted to bring Sparkle in for mine, but my mum said it would be too much for her."

"Who's Sparkle?" asked Lily.

"My new puppy."

"I didn't know you had a new puppy! What breed? How old? Is it a boy or a girl?"

Jasmine was very happy to talk about her favourite topic, and she told Lily all about Sparkle. "She's amazing. And she's really good at learning. She's quite naughty though. It's because she's so clever. She wants to be doing things all the time. I forgot to put her in her crate the other day when I went upstairs, and she chewed up all the socks in the washing basket. And she chewed up her puppy-sitter's slippers."

Lily laughed. She said goodbye to Shadow at the school gates and handed his lead to her mum.

Jasmine had made a PowerPoint presentation for her talk. The first slide said:

## What is a Puppy Farm?

Underneath the title was a photo of Sparkle curled up on Jasmine's bed. The class broke into a chorus of exclamations at Sparkle's cuteness. Jasmine waited until Ms Walker had quietened everyone down, and then she said, "A puppy farm sounds cute, doesn't it? But does anyone know what a puppy farm actually is?"

People shook their heads.

"They're places where people breed loads and loads of puppies just to make money. They make the poor mothers have litter after litter of puppies until they're exhausted, and they don't care about the dogs, so they're often kept in dirty sheds. They often don't have the puppies vaccinated or wormed, so they can catch terrible diseases. Did you know that one in

every five dogs that comes from a puppy farm dies before it's six months old?"

"That's terrible!" said Aisha.

"But why are puppy farms allowed?" asked Patrick.

"Save your questions until the end, everyone," said Ms Walker.

"They're not allowed," said Jasmine. "Everyone who buys a puppy wants a happy, healthy dog, so puppy farmers pretend they're kind, caring owners. OK, I'm going to do a quiz. Look at this online advert for puppies."

She showed an image of a litter of Labrador puppies. There was an excited babble of "Aah!" and "Ooh!" and "So cute!"

The text under the picture said:

*Beautiful litter of puppies for sale. Kennel Club registered. 8 weeks old. Fully vaccinated. Call to view.*

"OK," said Jasmine. "Put your hand up if you

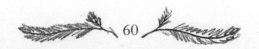

think these puppies come from a puppy farm."

A few children raised their hands. Some looked at their friends to see which way they were voting before they put their hands up. Rishi put his hand halfway up, wiggled it about a bit and put it down again.

"Now put your hand up if you think these puppies don't come from a puppy farm," said Jasmine.

Bella's hand went up, followed by Sadie's and Millie's. Other hands waved tentatively in the air.

"The answer," said Jasmine, "is that you can't tell. I made that advert, and I got the picture from the Internet. So a puppy farmer can easily do that too. The puppies in the picture might not be the ones they're actually selling. They might be lying about them being registered and vaccinated. So if you were thinking of buying one of those puppies, you'd need to ask a lot more questions. You should research the breed

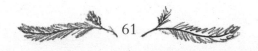

you want to buy and ask the seller about it.
A proper breeder would know loads about
Labradors. Also ask to see more photos. All
proper breeders take loads of pictures of their
puppies. And ask the name of their vet's practice
and then look up their website and phone them
to make sure they did actually vaccinate the
puppies."

Jasmine showed her next slide, a photo of a
modern detached house on a street.

"Imagine this is the house where you go to
buy your puppy. Put your hand up if you think
it's a puppy farm."

Two people put their hands up.

"Put your hands up if you think it's not."

Most people raised their hands.

"The answer is also that you can't tell," said
Jasmine. "Some puppy farmers use someone
else's house to sell the puppies from, to pretend
the puppy comes from a happy home. So
make sure you ask the seller lots of questions

and make sure they ask you lots of questions too. A caring breeder will want to know their puppies are going to a good home. If they seem very keen to sell the puppy and they don't ask you many questions, they're probably a puppy farmer."

She showed a photo of an adult dog. "If you're thinking of buying a puppy, you should always ask to see it with its mum and all its brothers and sisters. If the seller won't let you, that probably means the puppy has come from a puppy farm. But some puppy farmers use a different dog and pretend it's the puppy's mum. So how can you tell if it really is or not?"

Sophie put her hand up. "The puppies would be drinking their mum's milk."

"The puppies would snuggle up with her," said Lily.

"She would protect them," said Marco.

"They would want to play with her," said Tom.

"Exactly," said Jasmine. "So never buy a puppy without seeing it with its mum and watching them together."

Her next slide was a photo of Sparkle playing with a ball. Jasmine explained how she had got Sparkle and how Nadia had realised that she'd come from a puppy farm.

"The police and the local council are investigating the place she came from," Jasmine said, "so hopefully the owners will be taken to court. That's the end of my talk."

The class clapped.

"Thank you very much, Jasmine," said Ms Walker. "That was really interesting. Now, we've got time for one or two questions."

Bella's hand shot up. Jasmine looked warily at her. She and Bella did not get on.

"Yes, Bella?" said the teacher.

Bella tilted her head to one side and smiled sweetly. "You said people shouldn't buy puppies from puppy farms, but your puppy came from a

puppy farm."

"What's your point?" said Jasmine.

"So isn't it a good thing that people buy puppies from puppy farms?" said Bella triumphantly. "Otherwise the poor puppies would just get ill and probably die. Are you saying your puppy should have been left to die?"

She sat back with a satisfied look.

"That's a very good point," said Jasmine. "I'm glad you asked that question."

Bella looked confused.

"A lot of people think like that," said Jasmine. "They think if they buy the puppy, they're doing a good thing, by rescuing it from the puppy farmers and giving it a better life. But the problem is, if you buy that puppy you're giving money to people who are cruel to animals, and you're encouraging them to carry on breeding more litters from exhausted dogs who are kept in horrible conditions."

"So you should just leave the puppy to die?" said Bella.

"No. You should report the puppy farmers. If you saw the advert online, report it to the website it was on. Also, all puppy breeders need a licence, so report them to the local council. They'll check to see if they're licensed, and if they're following the rules. If you think they're not looking after their dogs properly, report them to the RSPCA. And if you actually see any cruelty, report them to the police. That should get them investigated and hopefully shut down, and their dogs will be rehomed. If everyone did that, puppy farms wouldn't exist any more, and all puppies would come from proper caring breeders."

"Thank you very much, Jasmine," said Ms Walker. "What a fantastic answer. I hope that helped, Bella?"

Bella gave a tiny, grudging nod. Jasmine could tell she was seething.

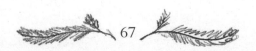

"Excellent work, Jasmine," said Ms Walker. "I'm going to recommend you to Mrs Allerton for a gold medal."

Jasmine stared at her, amazed. Ms Walker was known for being mean about handing out rewards, and Jasmine had never expected to receive a gold medal. She had only ever been in Mrs Allerton's office when she was in trouble.

But her biggest reward came when she saw Bella Bradley's face as she walked back to her seat. Bella looked as though she was about to burst with fury.

# Chapter Seven
## A Four-Legged Classmate

When Jasmine's class lined up in the playground on Tuesday morning, they were very excited to have a new four-legged classmate. Shadow the spaniel walked calmly into the room and lay down beside Lily's chair, resting his handsome head on her feet.

"We're extremely lucky to have Shadow with us this morning," said Ms Walker, "but we must remember he's a working dog, which means we need to stay calm and let him do his job. So no fussing over him or touching him, please."

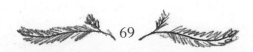

Lily led Shadow to the front of the classroom and said, "Lie down." Shadow settled himself beside her.

"Shadow is a fully trained medical alert assistance dog," said Lily. "I've had him since I was six and he's my best friend. I got him because I have type 1 diabetes. Anyone can get type 1 diabetes, and scientists still don't know exactly what causes it. There's no cure for it yet, but it can be controlled."

She showed a slide that said:

## What is Type 1 Diabetes?

"Our bodies produce a substance called insulin," said Lily. "Insulin is a hormone that controls the amount of sugar in your blood. But when you have diabetes, your body doesn't produce enough insulin, so you need insulin injections every day. And even then, your blood sugar can quickly become too low, or sometimes

too high, and that can make you very ill. Some people with diabetes have no warning signs that their blood sugar is getting dangerously low. I don't get any warning signs. If my blood sugar gets very low, it's called hypoglycaemia. When you have a hypo, you can faint, have a seizure or even go into a coma. Hypos can happen at night too, so my mum used to have to sleep in my room all night and get up every hour to test my blood sugar levels."

Jasmine's eyes opened wide. She'd had no idea that Lily had to be tested all through the night as well as during the day.

"That's where Shadow comes in," Lily said. "Everyone knows that dogs have an incredible sense of smell, but you might not know that a dog's sense of smell is a thousand times better than a human's. Dogs can detect smells better than any technology that's ever been invented. Their sense of smell is so good that scientists are learning from dogs how to detect certain scents

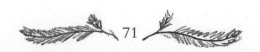

that no human or technology can detect at the moment."

Her next slide showed a dog sniffing a little tub in a row of identical containers.

"Shadow has been trained as a hypo alert dog," said Lily. "So he can smell when my blood sugar's getting too low, and he's been trained to alert me and fetch my medical kit."

There were admiring sounds from around the room.

"Wow," said Jasmine. "That's amazing."

"He's even learned to open the zip of my rucksack and take out my medical kit," said Lily. "Or if I'm out with my mum and she's carrying the kit, he knows and he'll fetch it from her bag."

She showed her next slide: a photo of her in bed with Shadow lying beside her.

"When we got Shadow, my mum could get a proper night's sleep for the first time, because Shadow could sleep in my bed. If my blood

sugar got too low, Shadow woke me, and he went and woke my mum too."

Lily took off her cardigan and showed the class a little white disc stuck to her upper arm.

"This is a CGM, which stands for Continuous Glucose Monitor. I had one before but it wasn't very accurate. This new one's much better. It monitors my blood glucose every minute, and you've all heard the alarm that goes off when my blood sugar gets too low. When it sounds, I scan the sensor to get a reading, and then I do what I need to do so I don't have a hypo. If I need help in school, Mrs Cresswell is trained to support me, and she's come to hear my talk."

Lily smiled at someone at the back of the class. Everyone turned and saw Mrs Cresswell, the school secretary, standing by the door. She gave them a little wave.

"So if you have that thing on your arm," said Bella, "why do you need Shadow?"

Ms Walker looked as though she was about

to tell Bella off for interrupting, but Lily said, "Well, I had Shadow for years before the new technology came out, and he's still the best. The sensor doesn't always work perfectly, and sometimes the reader runs out of battery, but Shadow's battery never runs out. Also, he's given me more confidence, and he's great for making me do lots of exercise, which is important if you have diabetes."

Lily showed a slide of various dogs wearing assistance-dog jackets.

"Medical detection dogs can sniff out diseases like cancer, which humans can't smell at all," she said. "Imagine if your sense of smell was so good that you could detect half a spoonful of sugar dissolved in an Olympic-sized swimming pool full of water. Dogs can detect diseases in such tiny amounts that it's the same as that."

She showed a picture of a woman in running gear, crouching down with her arm around a cocker spaniel wearing an alert jacket.

"Some alert assistance dogs are trained to help people with epilepsy," said Lily. "They can detect when their human partner is about to have an epileptic fit. This dog alerts her human partner exactly twenty-five minutes before she has a fit. No human can detect it. She can't detect it herself, but her dog can. She didn't used to be able to leave her house, because she never knew if she might have a fit in public and injure herself or even die, but now the dog is with her, she alerts her and she has enough time to get home or get to a safe place before the fit happens."

"That's incredible," murmured Mrs Cresswell. Jasmine glanced at her and saw to her surprise that she had tears in her eyes.

"Another dog alerts his partner exactly forty-eight minutes before she has a fit. He'll even run in from another room to let her know. The dogs get it right every single time. And that's why alert dogs are amazing. Thank you."

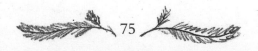

Everyone clapped. Hands shot up around the room.

"That was incredible," said Ms Walker. "We've learned so much this morning, Lily. Thank you for teaching us and sharing your experiences. OK, let's have a few questions. Patrick?"

"How do the dogs alert their owners exactly forty-eight minutes or whatever it is before they have a fit?"

"Nobody knows exactly how they do it," said Lily, "but they must be able to smell chemical changes that happen in their partner's body. Scientists are trying to learn from dogs how to detect these chemical changes."

"That's fascinating," said Ms Walker. "I love that scientists are learning from dogs. Julia?"

"Could you bring Shadow to school every day?" asked Julia.

"I'd love to, but he's on duty all night, so he needs a rest in the day. He walks to school with me, and then he goes home with my mum and

rests, and then he comes with her to collect me."

"Did you train Shadow yourself?" asked Tom.

"No, he was trained by Alert Dogs. We applied to them and they matched me with Shadow."

"One more question," said Ms Walker. "Jasmine?"

"How do dogs get to be alert dogs?" asked Jasmine. "Do they get picked out as puppies, and is it just certain breeds?"

"No, I go to training sessions at the centre and there's all sorts of dogs. Some of them come from rescue centres, or they're pets that need rehoming. They just have to love being with

people and want to please you by learning new skills quickly."

"Thank you very much, Lily," said Ms Walker. "I'll be recommending you for a gold medal."

Jasmine was thinking hard. A dog who needed rehoming? A dog who loved being with people, who learned new skills quickly and wanted to please?

*I wonder*, she thought. *I wonder.*

# Chapter Eight
## The Lady with the Labrador

At breaktime, Lily went to the office to meet her mum, who was coming to take Shadow home. Jasmine went with her.

Mrs Cresswell was sitting behind the hatch by the front entrance. When she saw the girls approaching she came out of the office.

"I so enjoyed your talk, Lily. And it was lovely that Shadow could come and meet your class. Isn't he beautiful? My dog died in April and I miss her so much."

"Oh, that's sad," said Lily. "Will you get

another dog?"

"I'd love to, and I'm retiring at Christmas so in some ways it would be perfect timing. But my husband's retiring in a year's time, and we're planning to go travelling, so I couldn't get one now."

"You could get one when you come back," said Jasmine.

"Yes, I'm sure I will. It just seems a long time away. I've always had a dog, and the house feels so empty now. Oh, here's your mum, Lily. Shadow can go home for a well-earned rest."

That evening, with Sparkle on her lap, Jasmine looked at the Alert Dogs website and found the page on rehoming pet and rescue dogs.

"OK, Sparkle, we just need to fill in this form, then someone from Alert Dogs will come and see you. Would you like to be an alert dog?"

Sparkle wagged her tail.

When Jasmine had filled in the form, she

went to the page on volunteering for the charity. She drew in her breath and looked up from the screen, her eyes wide.

"Oh, Sparkle! This could be perfect!"

On the first Sunday in December, Jasmine and Tom walked Sparkle to the village green to see the Christmas lights. Sparkle had had all her vaccinations, so it was safe for her to go to public places.

"It will be good for her to go somewhere busy," said Jasmine as they walked along the lane. "She needs to be socialised while she's young, so she doesn't get spooked by new things when she's older."

"We can do some obedience work on the green," said Tom, "now she's better at ignoring distractions."

"Guess what?" said Jasmine. "A lady from Alert Dogs phoned yesterday, and she's going to come and see Sparkle next Friday. Wouldn't it

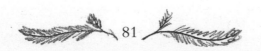

be an amazing thing if Sparkle ended up being able to save someone's life?"

"Look, there's Mrs Cresswell," said Tom. The school secretary was walking along the edge of the green with her husband. The Christmas tree lights twinkled and glowed, and fairy lights sparkled in the front gardens of all the houses.

"Oh, I wanted to talk to her," said Jasmine. "Let's go and see her."

Mrs Cresswell smiled at the children as they approached. "Hello, Jasmine. Hello, Tom. What a gorgeous puppy! Is she yours, Jasmine?"

Jasmine explained how she had become Sparkle's foster mother, and how Lily's talk had given her the idea of Sparkle becoming an alert assistance dog.

"And when I looked on the Alert Dogs website, it said they need more volunteers to be puppy socialisers. The socialisers look after a puppy for a year until it starts its proper alert dog training. And I thought that might be

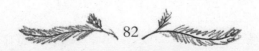

82

perfect for you, because you said you're going travelling in a year."

"A puppy socialiser?" said Mrs Cresswell. She looked at her husband. "That might be just the ticket, mightn't it, Stuart? I'll have a look at the website. Thank you, Jasmine. See you tomorrow!" And they continued on their walk.

"Shall we practise letting Sparkle off the lead and calling her back?" said Tom.

Jasmine hesitated. She had never let her off the lead in a public place, but Sparkle was very good at coming back when she was called now.

"Let's get a bit further away from the road," she said. "Over there by the Christmas tree."

"Look at that cute puppy," said Tom, pointing to an older lady walking across the green with a gorgeous black Labrador puppy on a lead.

"Oh, *so* cute!" said Jasmine.

"It looks about the same age as Sparkle," said Tom. "Maybe they'll be friends."

"Maybe it will be at the same puppy-training

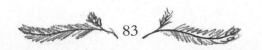

classes," said Jasmine.

"When's your first class?"

"Tomorrow. I can't wait."

At the Christmas tree, Jasmine let Sparkle off the lead. The puppy trotted around the base of it, sniffing excitedly.

"I wonder what she can smell," said Jasmine. "There must be so many scents around here."

"There's an RSPCA van," said Tom. "Why are they here?"

A white van with the RSPCA logo on the side pulled up on the verge. The children watched as two men got out. One of them walked across the green towards the lady with the Labrador.

"Excuse me, madam," they heard him say. "I'm an RSPCA officer, and we're searching for a black Labrador puppy that was stolen from a home in the local area. Would you mind telling me how long you've had your dog, please?"

The lady stiffened and took a step back.

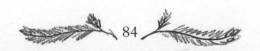

"Four weeks," she said. "Why are you asking? I hope you're not accusing me of stealing her."

"Of course not, madam, but the puppy we're looking for was stolen six weeks ago, and we have reason to believe she was stolen by the person who sold her to you."

"What? That's ridiculous. You've made a mistake."

"I'm sure the sellers seemed like respectable people," said the man, "but we have reason to believe they may actually be part of a criminal gang operating in this area. I'm sure you've heard about the increase in dog thefts. I'm afraid your puppy matches the description of a dog reported as stolen. We're going to have to take it while we investigate the theft."

"No!" said the woman, scooping the puppy into her arms. "I told you, you've made a mistake. There's dozens of black Labrador puppies around. How can you be sure it's mine you're looking for?"

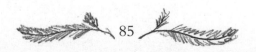

"I don't think that man's from the RSPCA," said Tom. "He's not wearing a uniform."

Jasmine frowned. The man was wearing smart trousers with a shirt and tie.

"They have those things on their shoulders with the RSPCA badge on," said Tom. "He doesn't have them. She should ask to see his ID."

"Tell her," said Jasmine. "Tell her to ask."

Tom hesitated. "You tell her."

"It was your idea. You tell her."

"OK, but come with me."

Jasmine's stomach squirmed as they walked towards the adults. She didn't want to confront this man, but what if Tom was right and he wasn't from the RSPCA?

"You're mistaken," the lady was saying. "I bought my puppy from a registered breeder. This isn't the dog you're looking for."

"Excuse me," said Tom, but he said it so quietly that she didn't hear.

"Excuse me," Jasmine repeated. The man

glanced at the children.

"Dave!" called the other man. "Let's go."

He was standing by the RSPCA van. He put something in the back, slammed the doors shut and headed for the driver's door.

"Apologies, my mistake," said Dave. He turned and hurried towards the van. The engine started. He broke into a run, pulled open the passenger door and jumped in. The van sped off along the village street.

"That was weird," Jasmine said. "Do you think he was trying to steal the puppy?"

"I took a photo of the van," said Tom, showing her his phone. "Look, you can see the number plate."

The lady hugged her puppy. "Well done for photographing it," she said. "I think you're right. We need to report them to the police."

"I'm sure they weren't from the RSPCA," said Tom. "They weren't wearing proper uniforms."

"Thank goodness they didn't get away with

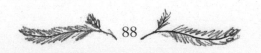

it," said the woman. "Though I can't imagine who would be fool enough to hand over their dog to a stranger."

Jasmine went cold all over. She spun round to look at the Christmas tree.

Sparkle wasn't there.

# Chapter Nine
## They've Taken Her

Jasmine turned hot and then cold again. Her heart pounded painfully.

"Sparkle!" she called frantically. "Sparkle!"

Tom ran towards the Christmas tree. "Sparkle, come here!"

Jasmine's eyes searched as far as she could see. There were children playing on the swings and slide, with parents chatting at the edge of the play area; an old man on a bench with a terrier beside him; Mrs Cresswell and her husband walking around the

perimeter; an elderly couple sitting by the duck pond; a group of teenagers lounging on the grass, and two women jogging along the path. But Sparkle was nowhere to be seen.

"Maybe she's by the pond," said Tom. "There's loads of trees and bushes there. She's probably sniffing under those."

"Is Sparkle your dog?" asked the lady.

"Yes," said Jasmine wildly. "They've taken her, I know they have."

"Let me help you search. What does she look like?"

"She's a golden retriever with a red collar. She's twelve weeks old. I know they've taken her, I just know it."

The lady put a hand on her shoulder. "Let's look everywhere on the green and ask everyone if they've seen her. If we don't find her, I'll call the police and report her missing, and I'll report that van at the same time."

"Call the police now," said Jasmine. "Please."

The woman nodded. "All right. I'll get the registration number from your friend. You two keep looking for her. My name's Zoe, by the way. And you are…?"

"Jasmine. And that's Tom."

Tom was walking around the pond, calling Sparkle. Zoe hurried towards him, while Jasmine headed in the other direction, her eyes searching everywhere, calling Sparkle constantly. But she knew it was hopeless.

All she could see in her head was the man shutting something in the back of that van. It was Sparkle, she knew it was. And now, while she was searching fruitlessly on the village green, the van, with Sparkle shut inside it, was speeding further and further away. And it was all her fault. How could she have taken her eyes off her puppy?

"Excuse me," she said to the group of teenagers. "Have you seen a golden retriever puppy?"

A few of them glanced up from their conversations or their phones for long enough to give her a blank look or shake their heads.

She headed to the playground and asked a couple of friendly-looking mums.

"No, sorry," said one of them. "We'll keep an eye out for her."

Keep an eye out for her! As if she was a mislaid sock or something! Did they not understand how urgent this was? Jasmine wanted to scream at them, but she just turned away.

She asked the other parents, and the man on the bench, but nobody had seen Sparkle. She walked to the far end of the green, calling the whole time, her eyes scanning the landscape.

"Hello, Jasmine," said Mrs Cresswell, as Jasmine approached. "What's wrong?"

At the sight of the kind, familiar face and the sound of her concerned voice, Jasmine broke down. She could barely make herself understood

through her sobs.

When Mrs Cresswell heard her story, she shot a worried glance at her husband. "Oh, my goodness. That must have been what you saw."

"What?" said Jasmine, staring at them.

"A man walked past us a few minutes ago," Mr Cresswell said, "holding something bundled inside his coat. I was sure it was a dog, because it was wriggling and I heard it bark. I thought it was strange that he had it all covered up. But he looked a bit stressed, and I wondered whether the dog was injured and he was taking it to a vet."

Jasmine felt sick. "That was Sparkle. It must have been."

"It might not have been the same man," said Mrs Cresswell. "What did this man look like, who was driving the van?"

Jasmine told her. She nodded, frowning. "It does sound like the same person. Oh, Jasmine, this is terrible."

Tom and Zoe approached. "I've reported everything to the police," said Zoe. "They've given me a crime reference number, for what it's worth, and they've said they'll get in touch if there's any news."

Jasmine told them what Mr Cresswell had seen.

"What vile, despicable people," said Zoe. "I'll phone the police again and let them know."

"But we should keep looking for Sparkle, shouldn't we?" said Tom. "I mean, we don't know for certain that they took her."

"Of course they took her," said Jasmine. "There's no one else here who's lost a dog, is there? And if it wasn't her, then where is she?"

"I just mean we can't be completely sure," said Tom. "She might have just run off. I know it's not likely, but it is possible."

"Is there anybody else you'd like me to phone?" asked Zoe. "Can I call your parents?"

"I'll call her mum," said Tom. Jasmine nodded.

She didn't trust herself to speak. Her eyes filled with tears again as she thought of her little puppy, alone and terrified in the back of a thief's van.

Mum arrived a few minutes later. Instead of being angry, as Jasmine had feared, she gave her an enormous hug.

"Tell me everything," she said.

When she had found out the facts, Mum agreed they should carry on searching for a while, just to make absolutely sure Sparkle wasn't on the green. Mr and Mrs Cresswell offered to help, as did Zoe.

"Let's meet back here in an hour," said Nadia, "if we haven't found her before then."

They swapped phone numbers and went off in different directions across the green and into the surrounding lanes, calling Sparkle.

An hour later a cold, dejected, worried group of people met on the green. Silent tears fell down Jasmine's cheeks.

"Maybe she walked home," said Tom. "Maybe you'll find her waiting for you when you get there."

Nadia gave him a grateful smile as she put her arm round Jasmine and pulled her close.

"Maybe," she said. "If she did run off, she'd certainly be able to find her way home from here. She'd just follow the scent trail back."

"Let's walk home now," Jasmine said to Tom. "We might find her somewhere along the way."

"Good idea," said Nadia. "It will start getting dark soon, so take the torch from my car. And if you don't find her, we'll start a publicity campaign. We'll make posters, use social media, everything we can to spread the word. We have to make it impossible for anyone to sell Sparkle without being caught."

# Chapter Ten
## Too Hot to Handle

Jasmine and Tom searched for Sparkle all the way home. They called her until their throats were sore, and they shone the torch beam in all directions, across the fields and into hedgerows and ditches. Jasmine knew she mustn't give up, and she was grateful for Tom's optimism, but she felt heavy with hopelessness. She was certain it was Sparkle who'd been bundled up in that man's jacket. And by the time they got back to the farm, even Tom had lost hope.

A robin sat in the hanging basket outside

the back door. He cocked his head, as if in sympathy, as the children trudged through the gateway.

"Look!" said Jasmine. "It's the robin who was in the house that time."

"Maybe he's a good omen," said Tom.

Jasmine wished she could believe that.

Nadia took one look at their faces and said, "You poor things. I'll make you hot chocolate. You need warming up."

While they were drinking their hot chocolate, they discussed what to do next.

"We can make posters," said Tom,

"and tomorrow we can put them up all round the village."

"Excellent," said Nadia. "Put my contact details on them – phone number and email. And I'll spread the word on all the local social media groups. I'll register her on the lost pets websites too. And tomorrow morning I'll get in touch with the local vets, dog wardens, shelters and charities. We need to make Sparkle too hot to handle."

"What does that mean?" asked Jasmine.

"It means making sure everyone in the area knows she's been stolen, so if the thieves try to sell her, people will recognise her and report them to the police."

"But what if they took her miles and miles away?" said Tom.

"Well, that's where the missing pets websites are useful. And I've already reported it to the microchip company, so if they get a request to transfer her ownership to somebody else, they'll

let me know. We'll do everything we can to find her."

Dad and Manu had been out on the farm all afternoon. When they came in for tea they were shocked to hear the news.

"Why would anyone steal Sparkle?" asked Manu. "They don't want to make a fur coat out of her, like Cruella de Vil, do they?"

"No, of course not," said Nadia. "They won't hurt her. They'll want to sell her for a lot of money."

"I'll put the word out around the local farming groups," said Dad.

"I know!" said Tom. "Let's print enough leaflets for the whole school. We can ask Mrs Cresswell to give them to every class to take home in their book bags."

"That's a brilliant idea, Tom," said Dad. "It's the perfect way of spreading the word around the village. I hope we've got enough printer ink."

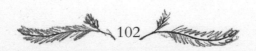

"Oh, Jasmine, you haven't eaten anything," said Nadia. "Try to have a few mouthfuls, at least. You need to keep your strength up."

But even the thought of eating made Jasmine feel sick. All she could think about was poor Sparkle, miles away in the back of a van. She knew everyone was doing all they could to find her, but her usual optimism had deserted her, and she was left with a horrible feeling in the pit of her stomach that she would never see her beloved little puppy again.

The evening was awful. Even though she was making posters and leaflets and planning how to get Sparkle back, Jasmine had got so used to having her around that she automatically looked down at the floor every few minutes, expecting to find the little puppy sitting on her bedroom carpet, gazing up at her. Then she would remember, and feel sick with horror again.

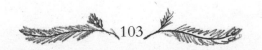

"I'll meet you half an hour earlier to walk to school tomorrow," said Tom, "and we can post leaflets in everyone's letter boxes on the way."

"OK," said Jasmine. She was reading an article on her mum's laptop about how to find a lost dog. Suddenly she put the laptop down and took an empty rucksack from a hook on her bedroom door. She started picking up discarded T-shirts, grubby jeans and old jumpers from the floor and stuffing them into the bag.

"What are you doing?" asked Tom.

"It's lucky I don't do what Mum says and put my things in the laundry basket," said Jasmine, scooping up a pair of crumpled socks. "These might be what brings Sparkle home."

"How come?"

"We should have thought of it before. Dogs follow familiar scents to get home. It says in that article that in perfect conditions they can smell familiar objects or people from more than twelve miles away."

"Wow," said Tom. "What are perfect conditions?"

"No wind, and cool damp weather. Like it is now. So we just need to leave scent clues that she'll recognise. I'm going to put her blanket in the farmyard – that must be the most scented thing in the house. And then tomorrow we can leave my clothes all over the village, and –"

She stopped as a thought struck her.

"What are you doing?" asked Tom again,

as Jasmine pulled the duvet off her bed, tipped the rucksack upside down and shook the dirty clothes all over the sheet.

"I'm going to keep these in bed with me tonight," she said. "Then they'll smell even more strongly of me."

Tom wrinkled his nose. "Nice."

Jasmine covered the clothes with her duvet. "Don't tell Mum. She might not want me leaving my clothes all over the village."

# Chapter Eleven
## No Time to Lose

Jasmine barely slept that night. She woke up very early the next morning and ran outside to call Sparkle. The blanket was still draped over the gate, where she had left it the previous evening, but there was no sign of the puppy.

Her head hammered with horrible unanswered questions. Where was Sparkle? What was happening to her now? Where were the thieves going to sell her? She imagined how scared and confused the little puppy would be, and tears came to her eyes again.

Jasmine dropped socks at intervals along the lane as she and Tom walked to school, and they posted leaflets through the letter box of every house they passed. They took the rest of the leaflets to the school office and asked Mrs Cresswell if she could give them to the teachers.

"We've put them into sets of thirty, one for each class," said Tom, taking out the bundles held together with rubber bands.

"I'll check with Mrs Allerton, but I'm sure it will be fine," said Mrs Cresswell. "It's a very good idea. I'm so sorry about it all, Jasmine. What a dreadful thing to happen. But she was microchipped, wasn't she? So I'm sure she'll be found."

After school, Jasmine and Tom took their posters to the village shops, and Jasmine deposited more items of clothing around the village. She walked home with a sick feeling in her stomach: half hope, half fear. Would Sparkle be there when she arrived? Might she have

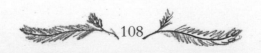

found her way home?

As she walked down the farm track, she saw her dad striding across the farmyard with Manu and Sky. She broke into a run.

"Has she come back?" she asked breathlessly. Sky trotted over and nuzzled into her leg. She ruffled his thick coat.

Dad shook his head. "Sorry, Jas. I wish she had. But the police phoned."

Jasmine's stomach churned. "What did they say?"

"They've checked the registration number, and that van has been reported by two other people in the past week, for theft and attempted theft of puppies."

Jasmine couldn't speak. Dad squeezed her shoulder. "It will be all right, Jas. You're doing such a great job of searching for her, and now you've got the whole village on the lookout. We know the thieves won't harm her, because they'll want to get a good price. And when they

try to sell her, the buyer will recognise her."

"Not if they sell her at the other end of the country."

"No, but the buyer's likely to get her checked by a vet, and as soon as the vet scans her for a microchip, an alert will come up saying she's been stolen. So we might have to wait a while, but it will be all right in the end. You'll get her back. I know you will."

"Thanks, Dad," said Jasmine. And although she was still scared and worried, Dad's words had calmed her down a bit. As she walked towards the house, she saw the robin perched on the gate, next to Sparkle's blanket, singing loudly.

"Hello, robin," she said. "Maybe Tom was right. Maybe you are a good omen."

The robin flew off the gate and settled on a nearby bush. Jasmine walked into the house and said hello to her cats, Toffee and Marmite, who were curled up together in their basket in the

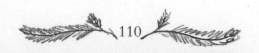

scullery. Toffee stood up and jumped down on to the floor.

"Yes, I'll get you some food," Jasmine said. But as she was opening the cupboard door, the phone rang. Her stomach lurched. Had the police got more information?

She dashed to the kitchen and snatched up the receiver.

"Hello?" she said.

"Oh, hello," said a man's voice. "Is that Nadia Green?"

"It's her daughter. She's at work. Can I take a message?"

"It's about the puppy she's lost. I think I might have seen it."

Jasmine's heart thumped. "Really? Where?"

"Well, I was walking my dog in Marlbury Wood this morning, over on the other side of Danstead, and I saw a golden retriever puppy with a red collar running through the wood."

Jasmine gasped. Sparkle had escaped! She was

on her way home!

"I thought it was strange," the man continued, "because I hadn't seen anybody else around. I met a couple of other people a bit further on and asked them, but it wasn't theirs. Anyway, it was a funny coincidence because I don't come to Westcombe very often, but I happened to go there this afternoon to visit my sister, and I popped into the newsagent's to buy a paper, and I saw the poster in the window about a missing puppy. So I—"

"Thank you so much," said Jasmine. She had a feeling this man might talk forever, and every minute spent on the phone was a minute when she could be searching for Sparkle. "Can you tell me the place names again, please?"

He told her, and she scribbled "Marlbury Wood, Danstead" on the notepad next to the phone. "And she definitely had a red collar?"

"Yes, I noticed that."

"Thank you very much," said Jasmine.

"Should I give you my name and number, in case Nadia wants to phone back?" he asked.

"Oh, yes, please."

She wrote down the details and thanked the man again. Then she raced out to the farmyard. There was no time to lose. She had to tell Dad and get him to take her to Marlbury Wood right now.

# Chapter Twelve
## On the Run

Jasmine and Sky sat on the back seat of Dad's truck as it rattled down the farm track. Manu was in the front next to Dad. He held a box of drawing pins and a pile of posters, still warm from the printer. If they didn't find Sparkle in the wood, they could at least put up posters.

"Don't get your hopes up too much," said Dad. "We don't even know if it was Sparkle he saw. There are probably lots of golden retriever puppies with red collars."

"It was Sparkle," said Jasmine. "I know it was."

"And even if it was her," Dad continued, "she could be miles from the wood by now."

"Sky will track her down, I bet," said Manu.

It had been Manu's idea to bring Sky with them. When he had suggested it, Jasmine couldn't believe she hadn't thought of it herself. She had done some scent work with Sky when he was a puppy, but then he had been trained as a sheepdog, and she hadn't done any more. Now she was using the journey time to do some intensive search-and-rescue training.

"This is Sparkle's ball," she said to Sky, holding the scruffy ball in front of his nose. "Remember this smell. Sparkle's smell."

Sparkle had carried that ball in her mouth so much that it must be drenched in her scent. Surely Sky would be able to recognise it in the wood?

As they drove further and further away from the village, Jasmine's heart began to sink. How would Sparkle find her way home from here?

Did she even have the stamina? She was only a puppy, after all.

The sun was setting as they reached Marlbury Wood. It was bigger than Jasmine had imagined, and there were several cars in the car park. There was an obvious main path through the wood, so they headed for that. Several people were walking their dogs along it.

As soon as they were on the path, Jasmine held Sparkle's ball out to Sky.

"Find Sparkle," she said. "Find Sparkle!"

Sky stood in front of her, eyes fixed on the ball, tail wagging hopefully.

"No, I'm not going to throw the ball for you," said Jasmine. "Find Sparkle!"

Sky looked hopefully at the ball. Jasmine repeated the instruction but he took no notice. She sighed with frustration and put the ball in her pocket.

"Find Sparkle!" she said, with a sweeping hand gesture around the wood. "Find Sparkle!"

But still Sky stood with his eyes fixed on her.

"Let's head along the path," said Dad. "Maybe he'll pick up a scent."

They walked slowly through the wood. The undergrowth was thick with brambles. What if Sparkle had become tangled in thorns and was lying there, trapped?

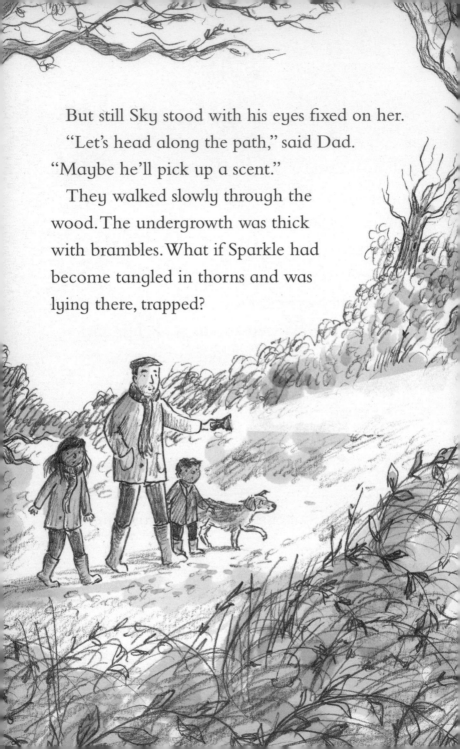

Jasmine kept calling her and encouraging Sky to find her. Sky trotted along in front of them, tail waving, sniffing at the ground. Had he picked up a scent?

It was growing dark. Dad switched on his torch and shone the powerful beam deep into the undergrowth. But there was no sight or sound of Sparkle.

At the end of the path, a gate led out to open fields. Had Sparkle gone through there?

Jasmine took the ball from her pocket again and showed it to Sky. "Find Sparkle!" she said. "Find Sparkle."

But Sky just looked expectantly at the ball.

"I don't think he's going to find her," said Dad. "I guess it was expecting a bit much of him."

"What are we going to do then?" asked Manu.

Jasmine felt an unexpected energy surge up inside her. She hadn't found Sparkle, but she knew she had been in these woods. And that meant she had escaped from her kidnappers. She was on the run, and Jasmine was going to make sure she found her way home.

"Our scents and Sky's scent will be all over these woods now," she said. "So if Sparkle tracks us to here, we can leave a scent trail all the way home. If you stop the car every mile, Dad, I'll

put up posters and leave a
scent marker in the hedge."

"What sort of scent
marker?" asked Manu.

"I'll think of
something," said Jasmine.

Which was why, when
they arrived home at
half past six, Jasmine was
dressed in nothing but
her underwear, shoes, and
a sweatshirt belonging to
Dad that came down to
her knees.

## Chapter Thirteen
# Sparkle's Christmas Stocking

The next morning Jasmine again woke early and ran outside, scanning the farmyard and calling to Sparkle. Surely she should have made it home by now?

But there was no sign of her. What if it hadn't been Sparkle in Marlbury Wood after all? Or what if she had been injured, or caught in a trap on her way home?

Jasmine turned cold. What if Sparkle had been run over? What if she had been struck by a car as she crossed a road following Jasmine's

scent trail?

She hurried back indoors, where Nadia was putting the kettle on.

"Mum, can you drive to Marlbury Wood on your way to work, please?"

"It's hardly on my way. It's in the opposite direction."

Jasmine was about to explain, when Nadia's phone rang. Mum looked at the screen.

"It's the police."

Jasmine stood frozen to the spot, her head in a whirl.

"Oh, that's excellent," said Mum. "Thank you very much for letting me know. That's great to hear."

Jasmine frowned at her, trying to work this out. If the news was excellent, why didn't Mum sound excited?

"What is it?" she asked as Mum put the phone down. "Have they found Sparkle?"

"No, I'm afraid not," said Nadia. "But it's

123

good news in a different way. The puppy
farmers who bred Sparkle have been arrested."

"Good," said Jasmine. "I hope they get put in
prison for life."

"I doubt that," said Nadia. "But they may
well go to prison, and they should definitely be
banned from keeping animals for life."

Jasmine's class spent the lesson before lunch
making Christmas decorations. Jasmine was
making paper snowflakes, which she normally
loved, but today she was unable to enjoy
anything. It was bitterly cold outside, with an
icy east wind. How long could a puppy survive
in these conditions?

As she and Tom were finishing their lunch,
Mrs Cresswell came into the dining hall and
made her way to their table.

"Jasmine, your mum's on the phone," she said.
"She asked to speak to you."

Jasmine turned hot and cold. Mum had never,

ever phoned her at school. She didn't dare hope it was good news and she couldn't let herself think about bad news.

Mrs Cresswell held out her hand. "Do you want to come to the office with me? Your mum's waiting to speak to you."

Jasmine's hand shook as she picked up the receiver.

"What's happened?"

"The police just phoned again," said Nadia. "They've caught the dog thieves."

Jasmine gasped. "Have they found Sparkle?"

"No. Sparkle escaped."

"When? Where?"

"The police traced the van to an address in Bilston. That's only a few miles from Marlbury Wood, so it could well have been Sparkle who was spotted there yesterday. Two men matching your descriptions were at the address, and when they were questioned, they admitted to stealing her and two other puppies. The other puppies

were at the property, but the men said Sparkle
had jumped out and run away as soon as they
opened the van doors."

"So where is she?"

"We'll just have to keep searching. I think
we should go back to the wood. We'll take a
different route and leave more scent clues. I'll
pick you up straight after school and I'll bring
more clothes for you, so you can leave the
ones you're wearing for Sparkle to find." She
attempted a laugh. "Another day of this and
you won't have anything left to wear."

Just as the class had settled down for afternoon
lessons, Rishi shouted, "Look! Snow!"

Heads jerked up and swivelled towards the
windows. Sure enough, a few little snowflakes
were whirling through the air.

The class went wild. People started screaming,
cheering and running to the windows. But
Jasmine stayed seated, rigid with despair. A

blanket of snow would cover the scent trail and make the landscape unrecognisable for Sparkle. And her little puppy would be all alone in a bleak, frozen world.

Ms Walker let them spend the last hour of school decorating the classroom. Jasmine stood at the window, miserably sticking snowflakes to the glass. Real snowflakes continued to fall outside, heavier and faster by the minute. Already the playground was barely visible beneath a thin white blanket.

Tears welled up in Jasmine's eyes. All was lost. Sparkle would never find her way back now.

Then, through the bars of the school gates, she caught a glimpse of something. The hairs on her arms prickled. It looked like... But it couldn't be. Could it?

She stared out of the window, trying to see in the dim winter light, through the curtain of falling snow. Yes, a little creature was definitely moving around outside the gates, sniffing the

ground and the metal bars.

As she watched, the creature started to
wriggle through the bars. Jasmine's heart
stopped for a moment. Then she ran to the glass
door that led out to the playground and flung
it open. The freezing wind hit her face and a
flurry of snow blew into the classroom.

"Jasmine!" called Ms Walker. "What are you
doing? Shut the door!"

"Sparkle!" gasped Jasmine. "Sparkle!"

The puppy raised her head and gave a little bark.

"Sparkle?" said Tom. "Was that her?"

"Sparkle?" echoed the other children, crowding into the doorway and jostling Jasmine.

"Where?"

"Is she back?"

"Really? Where?"

"No way! Has she come to school?"

"Look, there!"

"I can't see! Let me see!"

"Oh, my goodness," said Tom, pushing through the mass of children to stand beside Jasmine. "It's Sparkle! She's come back!"

The puppy broke into a trot. Jasmine ran into the playground. And there, running to meet her, was the wet, bedraggled golden retriever puppy. In her mouth she carried one of Jasmine's holey socks.

"Look!" shouted Rishi. "She's got a Christmas stocking!"

"Oh, Sparkle, Sparkle!" cried Jasmine. And with a joyful bark the puppy leapt into her open arms.

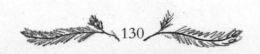

# Chapter Fourteen
## Happy Christmas, Sparkle

It was the best Christmas ever. Ella was home from university, Mrs Thomas spent the day with them, and Tom and his family came round for Christmas lunch.

Mrs Thomas was the first to arrive. She presented Sparkle with a beautiful basket of natural dog treats.

"I thought it might encourage her to chew on these instead of people's slippers," she said.

"Thank you so much," said Jasmine. "Don't they look tasty, Sparkle?"

Sparkle wagged her tail in agreement as she sniffed the basket.

Jasmine reached under the Christmas tree and pulled out a present wrapped in shiny red paper. "Happy Christmas, Mrs Thomas."

"Oh, Jasmine, you shouldn't have got me anything."

"Yes, I should. These are to replace the ones Sparkle destroyed."

Mrs Thomas laughed as she unwrapped a pair of purple velvet slippers.

"How thoughtful of you! Thank you so much. These are far lovelier than the old ones Sparkle chewed. I shall feel like a queen in purple velvet." She bent down and ruffled Sparkle's head. "I shall miss you, little Sparkle, even though you did chew up my slippers. It's been such fun puppy-sitting you."

"You can come and visit her with me," said Jasmine. "Mrs Cresswell said I can call round any time and take Sparkle for a walk."

"Oh, is it all fixed up?"

"Yes, it's amazing. We had the letter from Alert Dogs yesterday to say Sparkle's been accepted on their training programme. And then Mrs Cresswell phoned to say she's been accepted as a puppy socialiser and they're going to place Sparkle with her!"

"So it's all worked out perfectly," said Mrs Thomas. "I'm so glad."

"The lady who came to assess her had a massive list of questions," said Jasmine. "She couldn't understand why we all burst out laughing when she asked if Sparkle had shown any particular aptitude for scent work."

After lunch, they sat down around the Christmas tree to open presents.

"Can I give Sparkle my present first?" asked Manu.

Jasmine looked at her brother in surprise. She had no idea he'd bought Sparkle a present.

Sparkle had great fun ripping off the

wrapping paper. Eventually she tore off a big strip, and a box was revealed.

"A bubble machine!" Jasmine exclaimed. "What a great idea. Sparkle will love chasing the bubbles."

"It's not just a normal bubble machine," said Manu, almost bursting with excitement. "It makes bacon-flavoured bubbles especially for dogs!"

"Bacon-flavoured bubbles! That's amazing. Thank you, Manu."

Ella gave Sparkle a squeaky Santa toy, and Tom gave her a lovely red fleecy blanket and an interactive treat ball.

"You fill it with dog treats, and she has to push it around to make the treats come out of the little hole," said Tom. "I thought it would be even more fun than a tennis ball."

"It definitely will," said Jasmine. "Thank you so much."

Jasmine's present for Sparkle was so cute that she'd been tempted to keep it herself.

"Look, Sparkle!" she said, as the puppy gleefully tore off the wrapping paper. "Reindeer hide-and-seek!"

It was a red plush cube with holes in the sides, and into the holes you pushed little soft squeaky reindeer. "You have to bury your nose inside the cube and pull the reindeer out," Jasmine told her. "We'll see how long it takes for you to figure it out."

"Not long, I bet," said Dad. "I've never known

a cleverer puppy. There's not many dogs her age who could follow a scent trail for over ten miles to find their way back home."

"All thanks to my smelly socks," said Jasmine proudly.

Later that afternoon, when all the presents had been opened, the back doorbell rang.

"I think I know who that is," said Mum. "You go, Jasmine."

On the doorstep stood Mrs Cresswell, holding a bag of presents.

"Happy Christmas, Jasmine! I just wanted to pop round with these."

Nadia had followed Jasmine to the door. "Won't you come in for a cup of tea and some Christmas cake?" she said.

"Thank you, that would be lovely."

As Jasmine was about to close the door behind them, she saw a flash of red in the hedge.

"Hello, little robin. Happy Christmas."

The robin chirped a reply that Jasmine was

sure was his way of saying, "Happy Christmas to you too."

Mrs Cresswell gave Sparkle a set of rope toys for chewing, shaking and playing tug of war. "They're sold in aid of Alert Dogs," she said, "so I thought they'd be perfect."

She handed Jasmine a huge tin of home-made biscuits. "Without you, I'd never have had the idea of becoming a puppy socialiser. It's such a privilege to help train a dog that could end up changing someone's life. And it's even more special that I'll be helping to train Sparkle."

That evening, as she sat on the rug in front of the roaring fire, with the lights sparkling on the Christmas tree, Jasmine gathered the puppy into her arms. Sparkle had very much enjoyed playing with her new toys, but now they all lay strewn across the carpet, and she held in her mouth her favourite toy of all: Jasmine's holey sock.

"I'll miss you so much, Sparkle," said Jasmine. "But I'll come and visit you all the time. And you're going to train to be an alert dog! How incredible that you'll be able to change the life of someone who really needs your help."

Sparkle dropped the soggy sock and licked Jasmine's face. Jasmine laughed.

"Happy Christmas, Sparkle. It's been amazing to look after you. I can't wait to see what you do next."

# Acknowledgements

*While Alert Dogs UK is a fictional charity,
I was informed and inspired by the incredible
work being done by assistance dog charities in
the UK. This story is particularly inspired by
the work of two charities: Medical Detection
Dogs and Support Dogs.*